Sending Balloons to Heaven

by Lindsey Coker Luckey

Illustrated by Carlos Varejão

ISBN: 979-8-64-832379-7

It's been a whole week since I last saw my Mimi.
I miss her a lot but Mommy says that Mimi has grown angel wings
and is flying in Heaven now!

Mommy says that Heaven is a beautiful place and that we will all
see Mimi again someday.

Because Mimi is in Heaven, I can't talk to her like I used to. She was always so much fun to talk to. She and I would tell one another stories all the time!

I wish I could hug her again or snuggle up with her under her favorite quilt. I can still almost taste her yummy chocolate brownies. I can still almost smell her flowery perfume and I can still almost hear her laugh.

When I think about those things, I sometimes get a little sad. Lately, I like to lay in the warm, soft grass in our backyard and look up at the blue sky. I squint my eyes and try to see Mimi with her white wings jumping from cloud to cloud! She loved to laugh and play with me, so I bet she's still having lots of fun up there. I'm sure she misses me as much as I miss her too.

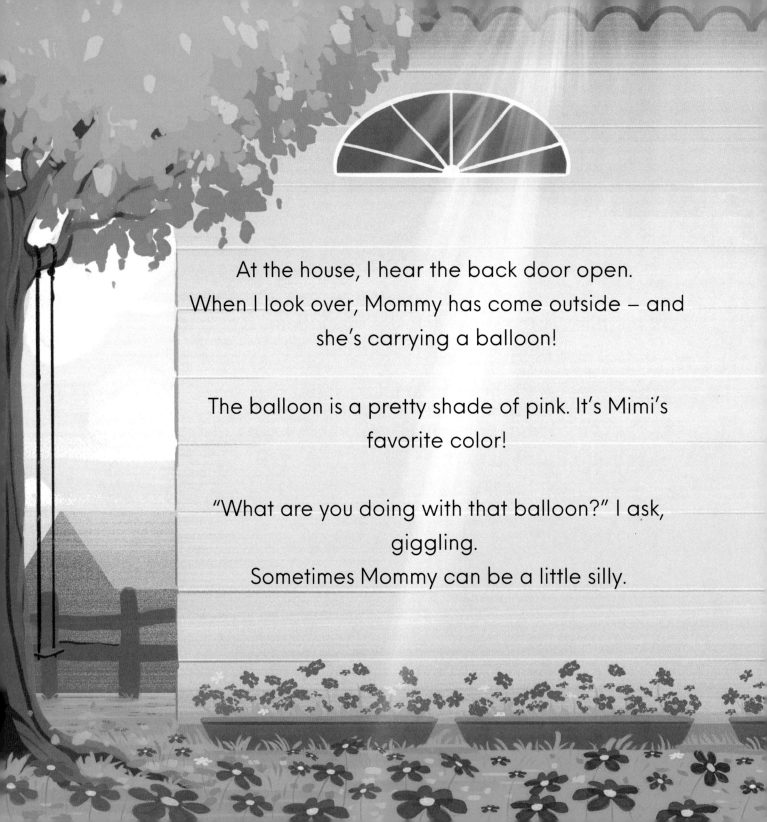

At the house, I hear the back door open.
When I look over, Mommy has come outside – and
she's carrying a balloon!

The balloon is a pretty shade of pink. It's Mimi's
favorite color!

"What are you doing with that balloon?" I ask,
giggling.
Sometimes Mommy can be a little silly.

Mommy grins and sits next to me in the grass.
She holds the balloon very carefully, so it
doesn't fly away.

"We're going to send this balloon to Mimi in Heaven,"
explains Mommy. "It will float higher and higher into the
clouds until it reaches her."
I gasp in surprise. "I can really send this balloon all the way to
Mimi?"
Mommy nods. "That's right! I'm sure she's looking down right
now, just waiting for this special gift!"

I touch the balloon. The pink color reminds me of the pretty pink flowers that Mimi planted all around our house. I still water them for her every day so that they'll grow so big and tall that Mimi can see them from Heaven.

Mommy tilts her head up towards the sky. I look up at the clouds too. The wind blows and it's nice and warm. Mimi used to say pretty days like this are a blessing. I bet she's really enjoying the view from Heaven.

"How do we know Mimi will get the balloon?" I ask.

Mommy winks. "Well, Mimi has angel wings now, so she'll fly over to
the balloon once it goes through the clouds. She's always looking over you to protect you, so she'll know when you release the balloon for her."

"Wow!" I say happily. "Do you think Mimi is a fast flyer?"

"The fastest!" Mommy answers with a laugh. "That way she can keep up with you while you're running around the playground or riding your bike up and down the street."

I grin up at the clouds for Mimi. I might not be able to see her, but I'm sure she's grinning right back. Even though I'm smiling, my heart feels a little funny. I'm happy that I can send Mimi this balloon, but I'm also still very sad that Mimi is gone. No one can tell silly stories in funny voices just the way she could, and I miss when she used to be able to tuck me into bed at night.

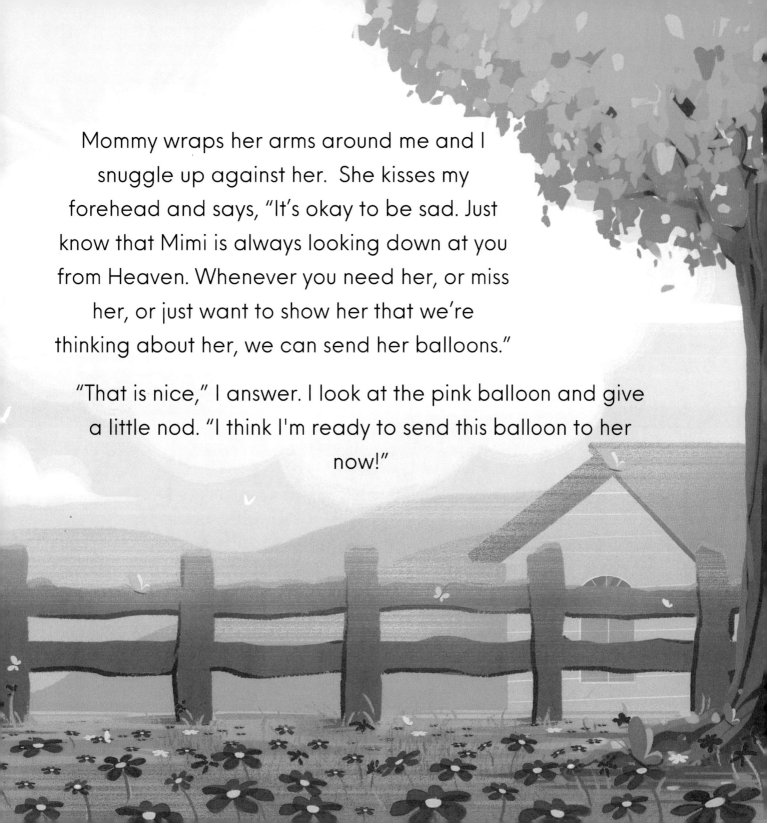

Mommy wraps her arms around me and I snuggle up against her. She kisses my forehead and says, "It's okay to be sad. Just know that Mimi is always looking down at you from Heaven. Whenever you need her, or miss her, or just want to show her that we're thinking about her, we can send her balloons."

"That is nice," I answer. I look at the pink balloon and give a little nod. "I think I'm ready to send this balloon to her now!"

Mommy happily hands me the balloon. "Whenever you're ready, you can let the balloon go!" she says. I hug the balloon against my chest. That way, when it gets to Mimi, she can feel the hug too.

Then, I let go.

The balloon begins to fly upward, just like Mimi must fly with her angel wings.

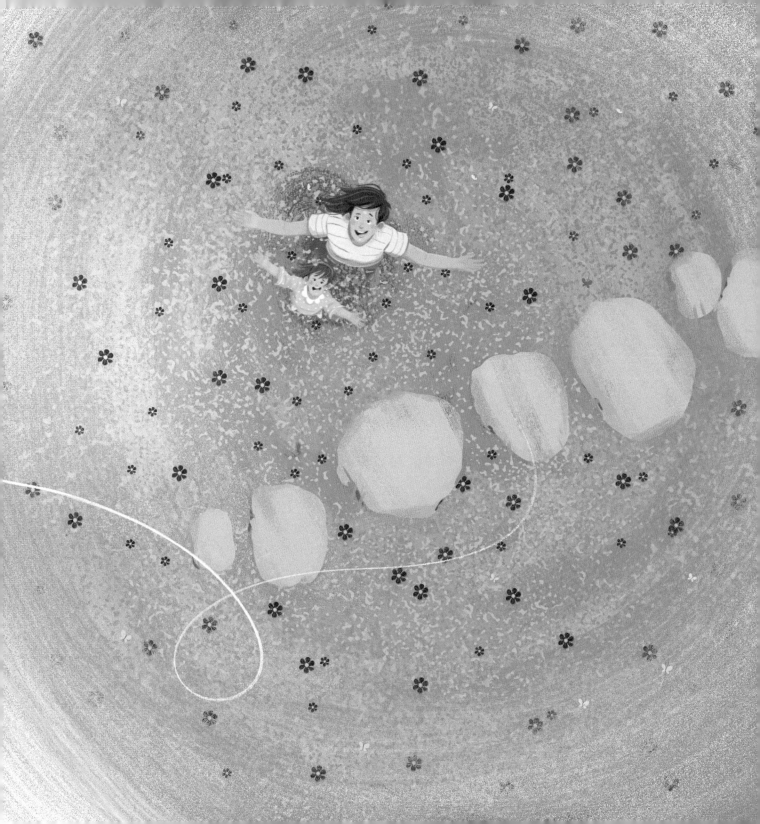

It bobs a little in the wind but keeps soaring higher and higher and higher. As it flies, it gets smaller in the sky and becomes hard to see. I tilt my head back and watch the balloon the whole way!

"It's almost to Heaven now," explains Mommy. "That's why it looks so little!"

Mommy and I keep our eyes locked on the balloon until it becomes a teeny tiny speck. A few moments later, it completely vanishes from view.

"I can't see it anymore!" I cry. "What if Mimi didn't get our balloon?"

"The reason you can't see that balloon anymore is because Mimi must have scooped it up!" Mommy assures me. "I bet she's feeling that hug you sent her right now."

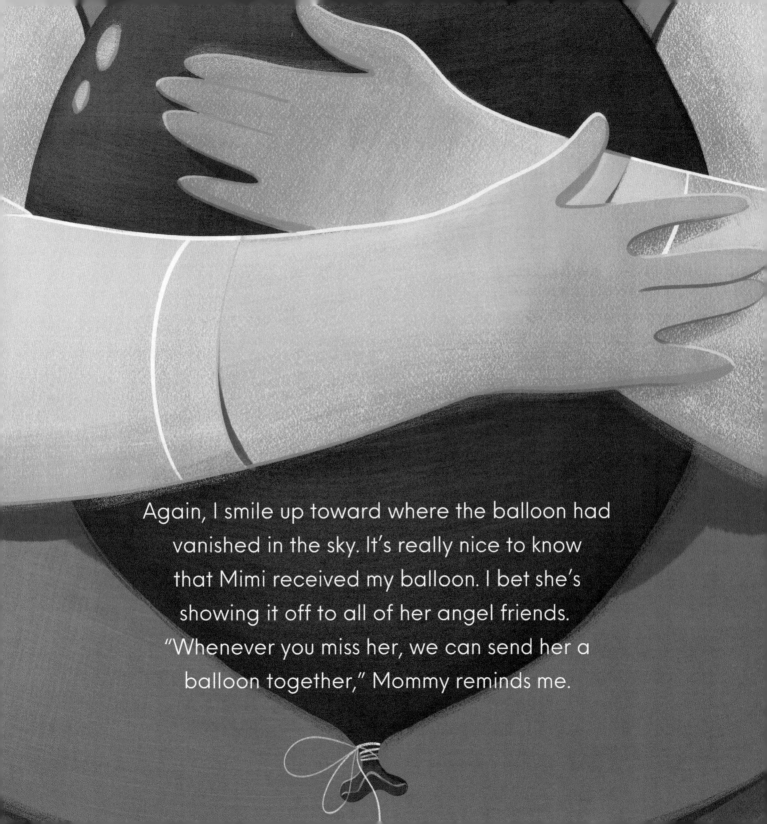

Again, I smile up toward where the balloon had vanished in the sky. It's really nice to know that Mimi received my balloon. I bet she's showing it off to all of her angel friends. "Whenever you miss her, we can send her a balloon together," Mommy reminds me.

Mommy and I lay back in the grass so we can watch the clouds for a little while longer. When the wind blows again, I think I almost hear Mimi's voice in the breeze. She must be responding to the balloon in her own special way. Mimi may not be able to speak to me directly anymore, but I can feel her in the sunshine. I can hear her in the birds chirping and in her flowers' leaves rustling.

Even though Mimi isn't with me, she'll never be all that far thanks to these balloons.

Made in the USA
Las Vegas, NV
07 February 2024